THUMB WRESTLING FEDERATION

OFFICIAL ~~HANDBO~~ THUMB

SCHOLASTIC INC.

New York Toronto London Auckland
Sydney Mexico City New Delhi Hong Kong

ISBN-13: 978-0-545-17661-3
ISBN-10: 0-545-17661-1

TM and copyright © 2008 The Larry Schwarz Company, Inc

Published by arrangement with the Thumb Wrestling Federation: TWF and Random House Children's Books, a division of The Random House Group Ltd

Published by Scholastic Inc. SCHOLASTIC and associated logos are trademarks and/or registered trademarks of Scholastic Inc.

12 11 10 9 8 7 6 5 4 3 2 1   9 10 11 12 13 14 15/0

Printed in the U.S.A.
First US printing, September 2009

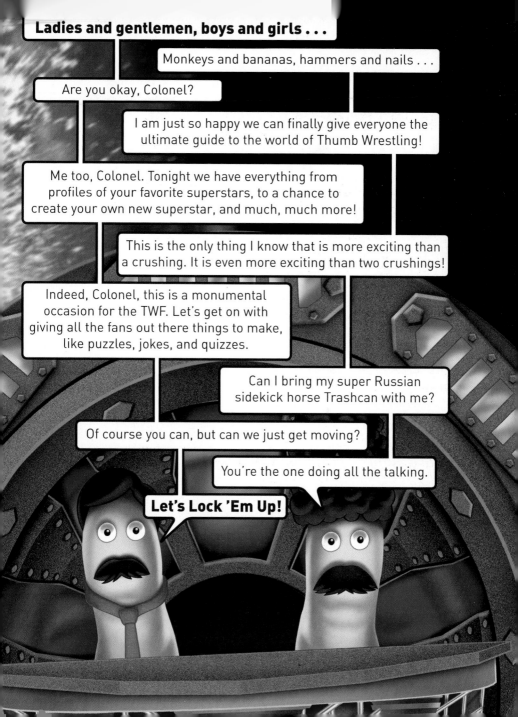

TWF: THE EARLY YEARS

★ ★ ★ ★ ★ ★ ★ ★ ★ ★ ★ ★ ★ ★ ★

Along time ago when wrestlers wore Speedos and had back hair, the four corners of the thumb wrestling ring were a place of heroic deeds, fair competition and honor.

The brackets were made, the bells polished and rung, and the scores kept; all by the wise thumbs of the Thumb Wrestling Federation. The TWF was presided over by Newt Knuckle, one of the sport's pioneers and its elder statesman. All was "A-OK, thumbs up!" the old-timers would say with a glint in their nails.

Thumbs up that is, until a young upstart named Pageboy Skull decided to change everything.

Pageboy Skull was a young man in a hurry. He didn't read the record books, and he didn't respect the old-timers – the greats who built the sport, like Newt Knuckle, Colonel Cossack and Phineas D. Finger. Pageboy Skull didn't want to work his way through the brackets by wrestling exhibition bouts in places like Thumboldt, Texas, and Thumbleweed, Montana. Pageboy Skull didn't have the time. He wanted it all and he wanted it now.

When Newt Knuckle thumbed his nose at Pageboy Skull's demand to be included on the Thumb Wrestling Federation's governing council, Skull led a revolt. In a tragedy that rivaled the Great Thumb Fire of 1881, the Thumb Wrestling Federation was split in two. Those with respect and with honor joined the "Mighty Dexteras." Those with less than a thimble full of decency joined the evil Sinistras. In the ensuing turmoil, Newt Knuckle and Phineas D. Finger disappeared, while other old-timers like Colonel Cossack threw in the towel.

Renaming himself to reflect his newly acquired status, Pageboy Skull became Senator Skull, leader of the Sinistras. As wrestlers battle to fill the power vacuum left by the disappearance of the TWF Legends, Senator Skull and the Sinistras will stop at nothing to defeat the "Mighty Dexteras," take over the Thumb Wrestling Federation and perhaps . . . the world! It's just a regular night at the TWF.

VINI VIDI VICTORY

Leader of the Mighty Dexteras

STATISTICS

POWER
AGILITY
STAMINA
LOOKS

PROFILE

"VINI VIDI VADA VOOM"

Vini Vidi Victory used to hang out with a rough crowd until he discovered the glory of being a good guy! The leader of the "Mighty Dexteras," Vini vowed that the Sinistras would never rule the Thumb Wrestling Federation! Armed with the determination of a true Dextera and a blinding right hook, Vini Vidi Victory will be victorious!

BIG STAR

POWER

AGILITY

STAMINA

BRAINS

As the cousin of wrestling superstar The Big Time, Big Star is wrestling royalty – even if he's not very cool or very smart. The Big Time was too embarrassed to let Big Star join the Sinistras, so he fights for the Mighty Dexteras instead. Big Star doesn't mind though, he just wants his cousin to be proud, and of course to be a big big star.

CAPTAIN ESPLANADE

POWER

AGILITY

STAMINA

ACCOUNTABILITY

Always outspoken outside the ring, Captain Esplanade gives off the confidence of a leader to impress his friends. While this Dextera may act like a hero, when it comes time to play his part in the battle against the Sinistras, he can usually be found hiding on the sidelines.

STATISTICS & PROFILE

STATISTICS & PROFILE

SENATOR SKULL

Evil Leader of the Sinistras

STATISTICS

POWER

AGILITY

STAMINA

SCARINESS

PROFILE

For some, being evil comes naturally. For Senator Skull, being evil is almost supernatural. He joined the Thumb Wrestling Federation as lowly Pageboy Skull and then impatiently revolted, splitting the TWF in two. Now, as Senator Skull, this evil mastermind leads the Sinistras. Victory for Senator Skull means the total destruction of the Dexteras, and complete control of the Thumb Wrestling Federation.

"EVIL IS MY MIDDLE NAME"

THE AMOEBA

POWER	
AGILITY	
STAMINA	
GLAMOUR	

Parties are a thing of the past for The Amoeba, who has put her wild ways aside so that she can focus on destroying the Dexteras alongside her fellow Sinistras. At least that's what she tells Senator Skull. In truth, The Amoeba uses her ability to shrink and expand to sneak into the hottest parties in town! This year, the big ticket is TWF and she'll do anything to make sure she's the main event!

BIG BAD BILLY GOATETSKY

POWER	
AGILITY	
STAMINA	
CRANKINESS	

Like the angry old man across the street who won't return your football, kid-hating Big Bad Billy Goatetsky is the grumpiest thumb around. Raised by goats in a petting zoo after being left there by his parents, Billy's sure to be butting heads with the Dexteras.

DANNY KABOOM

POWER

AGILITY

STAMINA

EXPLOSIVENESS

Tick-tick-tick-boom! Danny Kaboom is definitely a dynamite Dextera. Challengers had better watch out when this explosive wrestler is in the ring – Danny Kaboom can hit his opponents with all the force of an atomic blast. Equipped with everything from bombs to bazookas, this Dextra is ready to use his TNT to get a TKO!

STATISTICS & PROFILE

DORSAL FLYNN

POWER

AGILITY

STAMINA

HUMOR

Unsuccessful stand-up comedians don't usually stand a chance against a Sinistra in a fight, but Dorsal Flynn joined the Dexteras anyway! When Dorsal Flynn quit the comic scene to work out his routine with the good guys, everyone thought it was a joke. For better or worse, when Dorsal Flynn is in the ring the punch line is bound to be a gut buster!

STATISTICS & PROFILE

HOMETOWN HUCK
A True Gentleman Hero

DEXTERAS

PROFILE

Normally, being a good-natured kid from an all-American town doesn't lead someone to become a particularly powerful thumb wrestler. This isn't the case with Hometown Huck! Humility, honor and the ability to deliver one heck of a crushing, make Huck an exceptional fighter when it comes to protecting the Thumb Wrestling Federation from the unsavory grasp of the Sinistras! He may have left his farm long ago, but that won't stop this country boy from wiping the TWF stables clean with any Sinistra who dares to cross his path!

STATISTICS

POWER

AGILITY

STAMINA

CHARM

"SMALL TOWN, BIG THUMB"

BILLY BATBOY

POWER

AGILITY

STAMINA

CONFUSED

Billy grew up very confused and thinks he's a bat. With neither training, nor any real idea of how to fight, Billy Batboy relies on his costume to strike fear into any Dextera who crosses him. Unfortunately for Billy, his costume isn't scary, doesn't make him look like a bat and doesn't give him any powers!

CAPTAIN CARPAL

POWER

AGILITY

STAMINA

SEAWORTHINESS

Arrr! Captain Carpal is a pirate with the soul of . . . well, a pirate. After flying the Skull and Crossbones for years, Carpal found his true calling sailing under the Sinistra flag. Though his speech may be silly and his clothes rather smelly, this swashbuckler's out to make the Dexteras walk the plank!

THE BIG TIME

So Big, So Bad!

PROFILE

The Big Time has always been the best by being bigger than the rest! When his town got too small for him, The Big Time knew it was time to move on to the Thumb Wrestling Federation. He also knew that the Sinistras would be a perfect fit for his huge temper! Armed with a big thumb and an even bigger attitude, The Big Time is ready to crush any wrestler who questions what time it is!

"BIG ATTITUDE, BIG THUMB, BIG TIME!"

STATISTICS

POWER	
AGILITY	
STAMINA	
HUGENESS	

ROYAL THUMBLE

PART 1

Ladies and gentlemen! Wrestling fans and wrestling foes!

Puppies and kittens! Clams and oysters!

Folks, it's time for the wildest match in the wide world of thumb wrestling: The Royal Thumble Tag Team Championship! The winners of this match will reign as Royal Thumble Champions for an entire year!

Ladies and gentlemen, in this corner, a Dextera duo that's difficult to defeat: Face-Off Phil and Vini Vidi Victory!

VINI VIDI VICTORY
FACE-OFF PHIL

POWERHOUSE PAIR WITH SKATES OF STEEL AND FISTS OF IRON

POWER

AGILITY

STAMINA

LOCKER-ROOM LAUGHS!

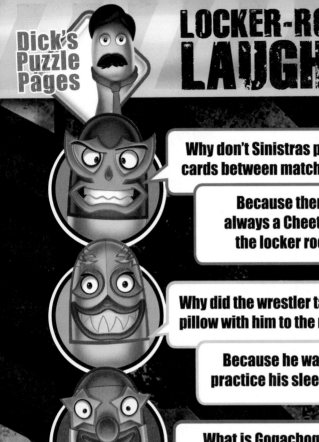

Why don't Sinistras play cards between matches?

Because there's always a Cheetah in the locker room!

Why did the wrestler take a pillow with him to the ring?

Because he wanted to practice his sleeper hold!

What is Gogachog's favorite food?

A club sandwich!

What is Sir Serpent's favorite subject?

Hisssstory!

TWF TEASERS

1 Which Sinistra has an evil plan to take over the TWF?

A. Corbata ☐

B. Senator Skull ☐

C. Hometown Huck ☐

2 She uses the power of rhyme to defeat her enemies, but who is she?

3 Which two Dexteras have gotten a little mixed up here?

1. _____

2. _____

4

A T A B B Y
B O G G E D
K I T S I L L Y

Rearrange these letters to give the name of a kid-hating Sinistra.

5 Who is the Russian commentator who often gets it wrong?

A. Fly Guy ☐

B. Dick Thompson ☐

C. Colonel Cossack ☐

▷▷▷ ANS ON P.

EVIL IRA

Zany Magician Trickster

STATISTICS

POWER

AGILITY

STAMINA

HYPNOTIC POWER

PROFILE

Born in a remote mountain village in Transylvania, Evil Ira has always been a weird guy! Not quite a magician, sort of a trickster, and kind of a hypnotist, Ira naturally took his eerie and odd talents to the Thumb Wrestling Federation! It was there that he was forced to adopt the name Evil Ira, after finding out that the name Good Ira was taken. Good or evil, Ira is certainly the trickiest Sinistra to get a hold on!

"WHEN TWO EYES JUST WON'T CUT IT"

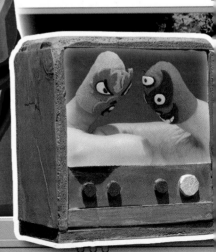

CHEEKO ROJO

POWER	
AGILITY	
STAMINA	
MISCHIEF	

The cheekiest of all the characters in the Thumb Wrestling Federation circuit, this Sinistra crony is always first in line to help devise devious doings. One thing's for sure, if Cheeko Rojo is involved, then whatever's happening can't be a good thing for the Dexteras.

THE CHEETAH

POWER	
AGILITY	
STAMINA	
HONESTY	

The Cheetah is her name and cheating is her game! This corrupt kitten would much rather cheat than fight fair – even the Sinistras know that nothing she says can be trusted. However, there is one thing the Sinistras do trust her to do, and that is to defeat the Dexteras!

FACE-OFF PHIL

Canada's Favorite Hockey Player

DEXTERAS

STATISTICS

POWER

AGILITY

STAMINA

SPORTSMANSHIP

PROFILE

Raised on the ice of Canada's countless hockey rinks, Face-Off Phil left a life of slapshots and snow for the bright lights of the TWF ring. A rising star who knows how to use a stick, Phil is sure to have the Sinistras against the boards this season!

"OKAY FANCY PANTS! TIME FOR YOU TO CHILL!"

FLY GUY

POWER	
AGILITY	
STAMINA	
PESKINESS	

Even his fellow Dexteras can't stand to be around Fly Guy for too long! He may not pack much of a punch in the ring, but Fly Guy's constant buzzing around and pestering should be enough to send the Sinistras running in the opposite direction.

GARY THE INTERN

POWER	
AGILITY	
STAMINA	
STYLE	

This Australian Dextera used to be a professional hairstylist. Looking for excitement, Gary found the Thumb Wrestling Federation. Gary helped the Dexteras with everything from photocopying to Band-Aid purchasing before he proved he could fight. When he's in the ring it can only mean one thing – the Sinistras are going to be sent Down Under!

CORBATA

POWER

AGILITY

STAMINA

MOVES

Video games know no worse punishment than the pounding of Corbata's thumb. After dominating the amateur, teen and professional video game circuits, Corbata moved out of his mother's basement and into the clutches of Senator Skull! Now a faithful Sinistra, Corbata will do all it takes to make sure that it's Game Over for the Dexteras!

DWAYNE BRAMAGE

POWER

AGILITY

STAMINA

INTELLIGENCE

This demented Sinistra may have taken a few too many blows to the head. He's a tough guy, but he's totally out to lunch, and no one can understand anything that he is saying!

STATISTICS & PROFILE

ITSY BITSY
Evil Spider Temptress

PROFILE

A classic thumb-eater, Itsy Bitsy is the heart-dropping and heart-stopping mistress of the TWF arena. As clever as a spider, this Sinistra will use all her leverage to devour any Dextera who dares tread near her waterspout. With a web that can ensnare any well-intentioned Dextera, Itsy Bitsy is one Sinistra to watch out for!

"EIGHT LEGS BUT NO FRIENDS"

STATISTICS

POWER

AGILITY

STAMINA

INTELLIGENCE

GILL

POWER

AGILITY

STAMINA

MUCUS

Gill has seen some dirty places in his time, but that's what he calls home. Moving from swamp to marsh to sewer to circus, Gill has always been a fan of grime and grease. When he joined the Dexteras, he made a promise to uphold a degree of hygiene in the locker room – as long as he was allowed to muck things up in the TWF ring!

GOGACHOG

POWER

AGILITY

STAMINA

INTELLIGENCE

This caveman from prehistoric times doesn't quite fit into this millennium. Gogachog might not be too smart, but he has the strength of a thousand stampeding buffalos, and he can crush any Sinistra into a million pieces!

MR EXTREMO
Daredevil Extraordinaire

DEXTERAS

PROFILE

Mr. Extremo takes it to the max, and then takes the max to the extreme! Whether it's a three-thousand-foot bungee jump from a helicopter or swimming in a tank of sharks, this Dextera daredevil will try any stunt once. Some things – like crushing Sinistras – he's happy to do a thousand times!

"TIME TO TAKE THIS TO THE EXTREME!"

STATISTICS

POWER	
AGILITY	
STAMINA	
FEAR	

CROSSWORD

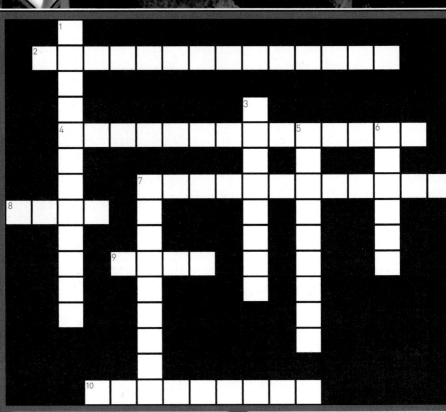

DOWN
1. He's just a good old country boy
3. The good guys of the Federation
5. Complete this phrase "Thumbs Up!. . ."
6. The samba-loving hothead
7. The Dexteras' evil opponents

ACROSS
2. Dick Thompson's commentary pal
4. The sport superstars take part in
7. He has an evil plan
8. Where Thumb Wrestling takes place
9. He lives in a swamp
10. Watch out for her webs

SPOT THE DIFFERENCE

If you want to be a ref in the world of Thumb Wrestling, you are going to need to sharpen your eyesight (despite what many of the fans think). Use your awesome visual skills to find the 11 differences between these two pictures.

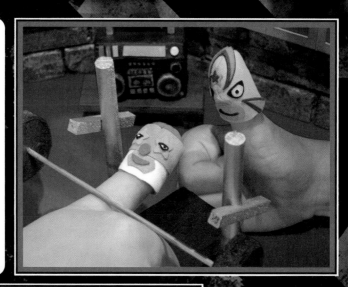

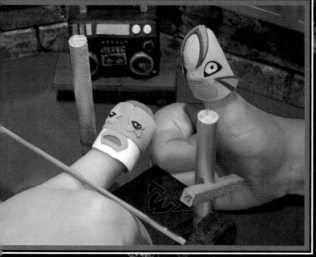

Ref's are well known for their excellent eyesight!

ANSWER ON PAGE 93 ▷▷▷▷▷▷

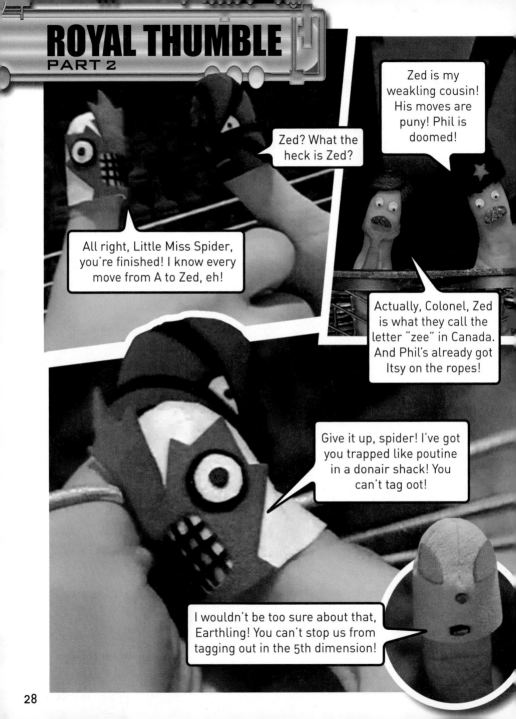

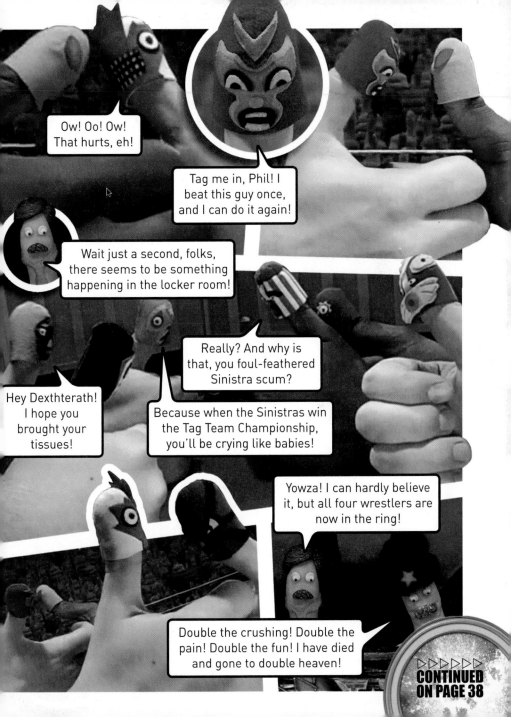

▷▷▷▷▷ CONTINUED ON PAGE 38

WASABI
Poet Laureate of the Dexteras

STATISTICS

POWER
AGILITY
STAMINA
RHYMES

PROFILE

Most slam poets don't actually slam – not so with Wasabi. She'll read you a poem and mash you into the ground before you can say "haiku"! It's tough for a girl like her to have to hang out with all the boys, but whatever emotions she can't get out on paper come out full-force in the ring! Any Sinistra who catches Wasabi on a bad day better learn to lose gracefully before this poet snaps and shows them who the boss really is!

"IT'S RHYMING TIME!"

JAMES MONTGOMERY FLAG

POWER

AGILITY

STAMINA

PATRIOTISM

Having a father like the famous Dextera, The Stash, was always a point of pride for James Montgomery Flag! Like his dad, James chose to wrestle for the good of the Thumb Wrestling Federation and to laugh in the face of danger! Danger, however, never laughed back at James and he has yet to prove himself in the ring!

KNOCKOUT NINJA

POWER

AGILITY

STAMINA

STEALTH

He's fast, he's furious, he's Knockout Ninja! After a life spent learning the deadly art of Ninjitsu, Knockout Ninja has taken his moves to the ring! He can vanish into the shadows and spit out haiku, but can he defeat the Sinistras?

N FUEGO

Nicknamed "Lance Romance"

STATISTICS

POWER

AGILITY

STAMINA

SPICE

PROFILE

"ARE YOU READY TO PLAY WITH FIRE?"

Hotheaded and samba-loving, N Fuego is the Sinistra that the girls love and the Dexteras fear. He can dance with the best of them and still take down a double-timing Dextera before the party's over. After being too hot for his own town, he took up with the Sinistras, where he learned to unleash his talents in the TWF ring!

FLASHBACK

POWER	
AGILITY	
STAMINA	
CLARITY	

Not much is known about Flashback's past. Mostly, this is because he's forgotten it! With plenty of evil determination but a sparse memory, Flashback is dangerous if he remembers that he's in the ring with a Dextera. Fortunately for the good guys, Flashback usually forgets he's even in a fight.

LAUGHING LOONY

POWER	
AGILITY	
STAMINA	
AMUSED	

There's something very creepy about Laughing Loony and his ceaseless demonic laugh. This sinful Sinistra seems to ooze evil, and his wicked right hook makes him someone that the Dexteras would be wise to avoid. One thing's for sure, when this creep is in the ring it's no laughing matter!

MAHI MAHI MINDY

POWER

AGILITY

STAMINA

ACTIVISM

Impossibly dedicated and invariably outspoken, Mahi Mahi Mindy's on a marine-life conservation mission that makes her one of the most passionate Dexteras. With the power of the ocean's bounty behind her, Mindy will make the Sinistras feel like fish out of water!

MISS FITWELL

POWER

AGILITY

STAMINA

EXERCISES

A doctor's note won't excuse you from the ring with this former gym teacher – Miss Fitwell knows a slacker when she sees one! This Dextera will whip the Sinistras into shape, and make them run laps until they drop down to the ground!

MILTY THE CLOWN

POWER

AGILITY

STAMINA

HUMOUR

You don't want to underestimate Milty the Clown. This silly old fellow takes comedy very seriously and considers laughter the strongest weapon! He may be full of jokes, but his skills in the ring are no laughing matter!

OUCH

POWER

AGILITY

STAMINA

CLUMSINESS

Being the Dexteras' top bruiser is a tough job for Ouch. He could be a good fighter, but somehow his clumsiness always seems to get in the way and he can never manage to get a break – unless it's his back that's breaking. Bandaged up and ready to go, Ouch is willing to take one for the team!

THE LOST VIKING

POWER
AGILITY
STAMINA
BRUTALITY

The Lost Viking will run you over like a freight train . . . and then ask you what a freight train is! The Sinistras found this ancient warrior frozen in a glacier and taught him their evil ways. Believing that Senator Skull is his true leader, he will do whatever is required of him. He's still confused about modern life, but boy can he fight!

MUGSY THUMBSCREW

POWER
AGILITY
STAMINA
RACKETEERING

You get a lot more than just Mugsy when this master mobster is in the ring. With his own gang of henchmen by his side, Mugsy is the most dangerous gangster in professional wrestling! Make him angry, and you might get whacked!

BUCKS GAZILLION

SINISTRAS

Billionaire Bad Guy

PROFILE

Billionaire businessman Bucks Gazillion has the best training money can buy, and a stunt double to boot. Only time will tell what this eccentric entrepreneur has in store for the TWF! Having dispatched many tough Dexteras, he now has his sights set on the ultimate prize – the TWF Championship.

"MAY THE RICHEST WRESTLER WIN!"

STATISTICS

POWER	
AGILITY	
STAMINA	
CASH	

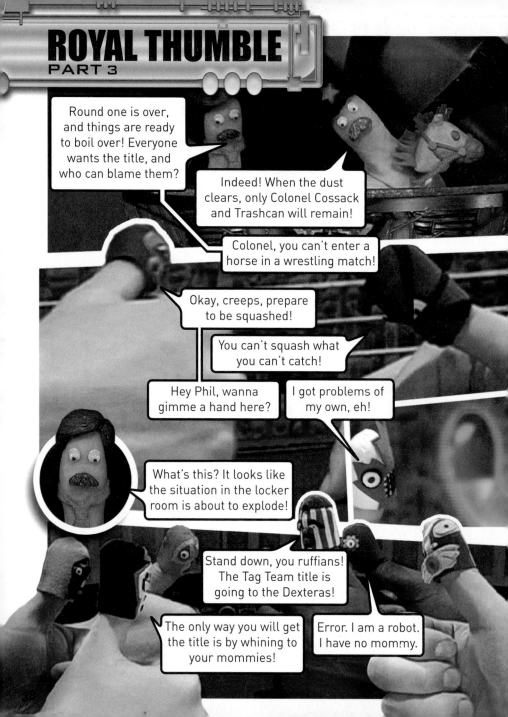

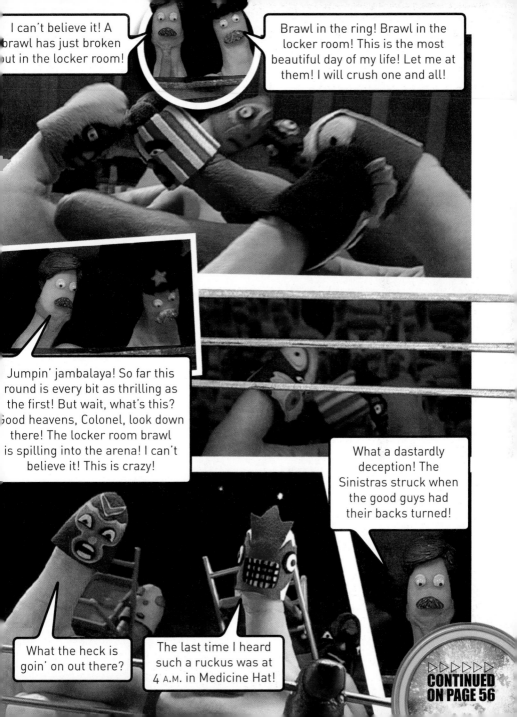

CONTINUED ON PAGE 56

Do svidania, weaklings! Welcome to your first day at the Thumb Wrestling Federation boot camp. I, Colonel Cossack, will draw upon my years of experience in the ring to make you into the most knuckle-cracking, digit-destroying wrestler around.

TRAINING CAMP

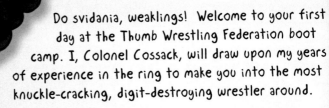

Enter the ring, then after your customary taunts it's time to lock up for the match. Take your right (or left) hand and lock fingers with your opponent, keeping your thumb at the top.

Before you can start the match, you have to give the traditional cry of, "Four, three, two, one, who will be the strongest thumb?" This must be done while waving your thumb from side to side in the opposite direction to your opponent's.

The match is on and it's time to prove your skills. Do everything you can to get your thumb above your rival's.

When, after much battling, you finally manage to get your thumb over your opponent's, what should you do next? Go for the final crushing blow of course! Bring your thumb down and try to pin your opponent's digit underneath yours.

Even though you have it pinned, the match is not over until you can hold it there for the length of the officially sanctioned TWF chant, "Four, three, two, one, I am the strongest thumb."

Well done, weakling in TV land, you are now a thumb wrestler! But don't go thinking you can compete in the dangerous world of thumb wrestling just yet. Practice and training are the key to making you a superstar. Remember, practice all your moves as often as you can and if you still can't win, maybe the Sinistras can help you out.

Whiteboard

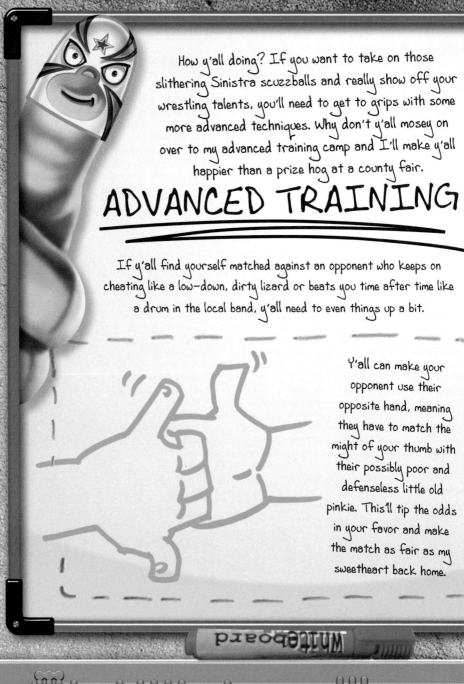

How y'all doing? If you want to take on those slithering Sinistra scuzzballs and really show off your wrestling talents, you'll need to get to grips with some more advanced techniques. Why don't y'all mosey on over to my advanced training camp and I'll make y'all happier than a prize hog at a county fair.

ADVANCED TRAINING

If y'all find yourself matched against an opponent who keeps on cheating like a low-down, dirty lizard or beats you time after time like a drum in the local band, y'all need to even things up a bit.

Y'all can make your opponent use their opposite hand, meaning they have to match the might of your thumb with their possibly poor and defenseless little old pinkie. This'll tip the odds in your favor and make the match as fair as my sweetheart back home.

Whiteboard

Thumb wrestling between two players is the most beautiful sight to behold, but y'all can kick things up a notch by having tag matches and rumbles.

Gill stinks of fish!

Tag matches can involve three or more players. All the players lock their hands together and wrestlers "tag" each other in to fight by tapping thumbs.

A rumble is an every-man-for-himself match. Again, players link hands and the winner is the one who can get the most pins in. Special rumble rules mean that if a player is already being pinned, the others have to stand back until the pin is complete. Of course those sneaky Sinistras have been known to try and slide in at the last second and steal a pin.

Make up your own mixes of matches — a Dextera's favorite is to have chain matches with players being knocked out when they are pinned until only one wrestler is left standing. Try some of the combinations shown here and organize your own epic bouts.

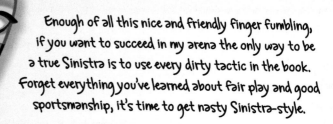

Enough of all this nice and friendly finger fumbling, if you want to succeed in my arena the only way to be a true Sinistra is to use every dirty tactic in the book. Forget everything you've learned about fair play and good sportsmanship, it's time to get nasty Sinistra-style.

SINISTRA SPECIALS

If you find yourself getting pinned all the time, you either need to go and join the Dexteras or try this little move I like to call "Death from Above."

Bend your thumb back towards yourself as far as you can. This will not only make your thumb taller and harder to pin, but will also make your opponent stretch to try and beat you, leaving them open to a crushing defeat thanks to your superior size. Don't forget to add to your opponent's shame by crying, "Death from Above!" as you deliver the deadly blow.

Whiteboard

An almost-guaranteed winner in any match is to unleash the Sinistra Sneak Attack. This takes some cunning and a little bit of lying, but as long as you win, who cares?

When you lock-up hands, tell your opponent you have a sore finger and cannot bend it. Keep your index finger out of the lock-up and put it to the side of your opponent's hand.

When your opponent least expects it, bring your index finger over and push down your rival's thumb. As you do this, bring down your thumb and watch the shame on your opponent's face as you pin him for the win, sneaky Sinistra-style.

To be a true Sinistra, you have to take your cheating to the next level and crush all who stand before you to dust. Only true evildoers resort to this final tactic but it is the only way to be considered a true naughty and nasty Sinistra.

The best way to win any match is to distract your opponent. This can be done in many ways and causes your rival to relax his or her muscles, allowing you to move in for a completely undeserved pin.

Oh yeah, I'm big!

Our favorite distraction techniques are:

- "Accidentally" knocking your opponent's foot under the table.

- Fake sneezing into your opponent's direction.

- Pretending to have a coughing fit, then slamming home the pin when your opponent least expects it.

THE SCORCHION

POWER	
AGILITY	
STAMINA	
VENOM	

At local desert dirt-ring thumb-wrestling clubs, the Scorchion learned to fight like a loner. He was never much of a showman, but word of his poisonous pinky soon spread and the Sinistras bagged him up as soon as they came across him on the highway. Now, this scorpion-like fighter wants one thing and one thing only: to deliver a deadly sting to the Dexteras!

SCOUTMASTER SCOTT

POWER	
AGILITY	
STAMINA	
MERITLESS BADGES	

Scoutmaster Scott's Cookie Scouts are no ordinary troop. These little evildoers are known for meritless deeds, like dumping trash on the highway and starting forest fires. They may not know how to make good cookies, but Scott and his scouts do know every wilderness survival trick in the book, and they aren't afraid to use them in the ring!

SICK VICK

POWER

AGILITY

STAMINA

GERMS

AH-CHOO! Watch out for Sick Vick and his flying bogies! This sick Sinistra has had an uncommon cold for his whole wrestling career, and he's famous for sneezing all over his opponents. In the ring, Sick Vick really puts the muck in mucus!

SIR SERPENT

POWER

AGILITY

STAMINA

ETIQUETTE

Knighted by the King and dated by the Queen, Sir Serpent is truly British royalty. After being exiled from the Royal Navy, Sir Serpent joined the Thumb Wrestling Federation and immediately the Dexteras learned to fear him. Though he may be incredibly well mannered, Sir Serpent is not above a slimy, slithering, sneak attack!

PEI PEI THE PURPLE PANDA

POWER

AGILITY

STAMINA

BEAUTY

Pei Pei is the Dexteras's beautiful prizefighting princess! Born and raised in a palace in Porpoisestan, she has pleased audiences around the world with her acrobatics. Don't be fooled by her grace and charm, this Purple Panda packs a punch!

PIERRE PAMPLEMOUSSÉ

POWER

AGILITY

STAMINA

GASTRONOMY

Pierre Pamplemousse's performance in the kitchen and in the wrestling ring will blow you away! He has traveled the world to gather the deadliest recipes around, and he has proven himself a true master of "ze art of gourmet combat."

UNIT 19G

POWER	
AGILITY	
STAMINA	
RAM	

No one really knows who built this wrestling robot, but they must have had a sense of humor! With enough bells and whistles to make a locomotive jealous, Unit 19G is a strong addition to the Dexteras. Unit 19G also seems to be programmed particularly well for dancing!

WEREDOG

POWER	
AGILITY	
STAMINA	
SLOBBER	

He may seem like a pretty average guy, but Weredog hides a big secret. When the full moon comes out, this otherwise friendly fighter transforms into a big furry dog. The Mighty Dexteras think he's lovable, but he sends the Sinistras running scared!

QUEEN NEFERCREEPY

POWER

AGILITY

STAMINA

ATTITUDE

The Dexteras are going to have to watch out for this creepy addition to the Sinistras's ranks. She's Queen Nefercreepy, the Ancient Egyptian queen of mean, and she's come to redefine the meaning of evil! Get on her nerves and she'll curse you into submission!

ROLF THE REAPER

POWER

AGILITY

STAMINA

ANGST

Only the impenetrable gloom of a rainy day can make this Sinistra feel at ease. Rolf the Reaper is one downer of a Deutschlander, and he brings new meaning to the word meaninglessness!

SNAGGLEFANGS

POWER	
AGILITY	
STAMINA	
APPETITE	

He eats everything. Everything!
With a seemingly unstpable appetite
Snagglefangs wsherything
he can get er
leave sma
danger

THE VISITOR

POWER	
AGILITY	
STAMINA	
STREET SMARTS	

No one knew what The Visitor was up to
when he landed on Earth, but Senator
Skull quickly took a liking to his dastardly and
destructive doings. It turns out that after growing
tired of ruling his home planet, he came here to
conquer Earth and subdue its inhabitants. Every
time this alien menace flies into the ring, the
fate of the Earth hangs in the balance!

TOM CAT

POWER

AGILITY

STAMINA

CURIOSITY

He's a little bashful and very inquisitive, but it's that curiosity that led Tom Cat to the doors of the TWF arena, where he met the Dexteras. Medical scientists still don't know how he can produce hairballs twice the size of his body weight, but they can't wait to watch him cough one up on the Sinistras!

TOM ZOMBIE

POWER

AGILITY

STAMINA

WARNING!
NEVER ALLOW
TOM CAT TO DRINK
ZOMBIE JUICE

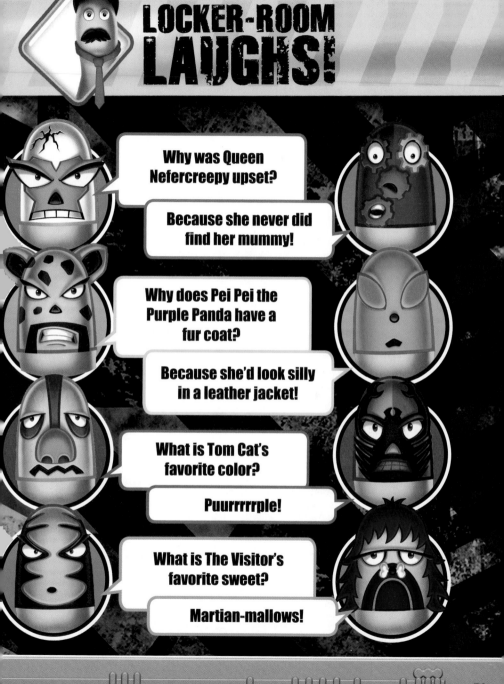

LOCKER-ROOM LAUGHS!

Why was Queen Nefercreepy upset?

Because she never did find her mummy!

Why does Pei Pei the Purple Panda have a fur coat?

Because she'd look silly in a leather jacket!

What is Tom Cat's favorite color?

Puurrrrrrple!

What is The Visitor's favorite sweet?

Martian-mallows!

TWF TEASERS

1
Which Dextera is happiest when sitting in a swamp?

2
He leads the Dexteras, but what is his name?

A. Pei Pei the Purple Panda ☐

B. Dwayne Bramage ☐

C. Vini Vidi Victory ☐

4
One is a prize-fighting princess, the other never stops laughing. Who are they?

1.

2.

3
The Big Time also has a wrestling cousin. Can you name him?

5
Which sneaky Sinistra uses webs as a weapon?

A. Fly Guy ☐

B. Itsy Bitsy ☐

C. Corbata ☐

PUZZLE POSER

It's been a busy day in the TWF publicity department and things have gone a little wrong with the latest poster. Use your skills to help the hardworking designers find the missing pieces.

▷▷▷▷▷ ANSWERS ON PAGE 93

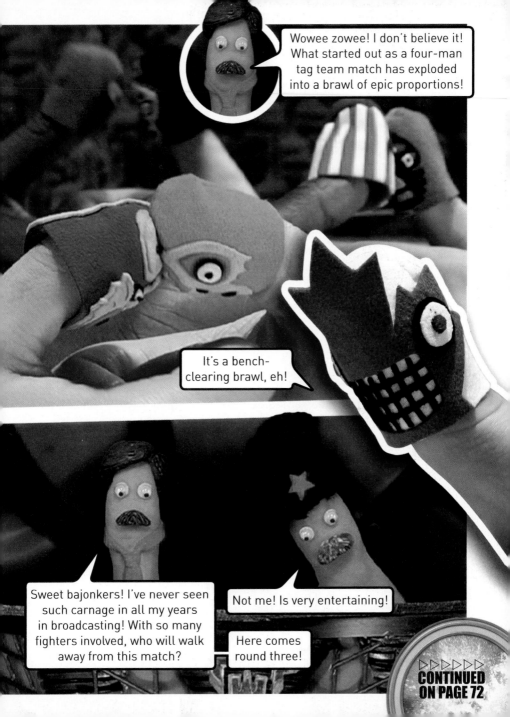

CONTINUED ON PAGE 72

BUILD-A-RING

Backyard thumb wrestling is all well and good, but if you ever want to see your thumb in lights and mix it up with the superstars of the TWF you are going to need to get in plenty of ring time. A few simple steps will see you throwing down with the best of them in your very own, officially sanctioned thumb wrestling ring!

YOU WILL NEED

- 1 piece of cardboard measuring 26 inches x 11 inches
- 6 pieces of white paper
- 5 feet of strong string or cord
- Scissors • Glue • Pencil

Visit the website and download the ring ends and ring cover files.

www.thumbwrestlingfederation.com/ring/

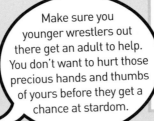

Make sure you younger wrestlers out there get an adult to help. You don't want to hurt those precious hands and thumbs of yours before they get a chance at stardom.

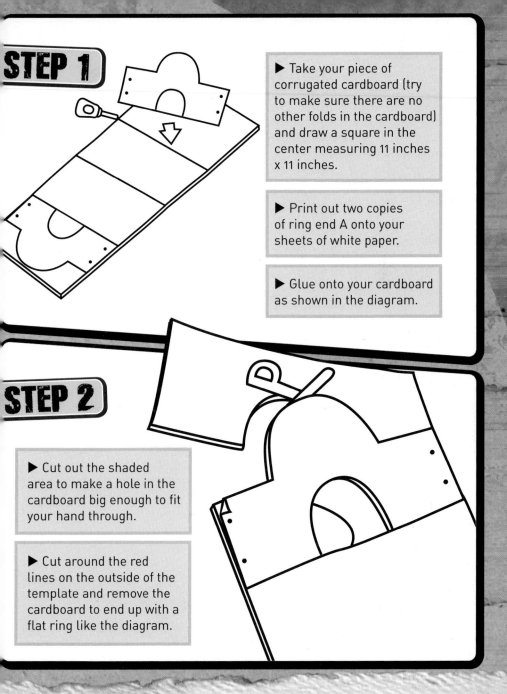

STEP 1

▶ Take your piece of corrugated cardboard (try to make sure there are no other folds in the cardboard) and draw a square in the center measuring 11 inches x 11 inches.

▶ Print out two copies of ring end A onto your sheets of white paper.

▶ Glue onto your cardboard as shown in the diagram.

STEP 2

▶ Cut out the shaded area to make a hole in the cardboard big enough to fit your hand through.

▶ Cut around the red lines on the outside of the template and remove the cardboard to end up with a flat ring like the diagram.

STEP 3

▶ Turn your cardboard over so the ring mat is facing up again.

▶ Make holes through the cardboard using a pencil to push through the red circles on the ring ends.

▶ Place a ruler along the bottom edge of the ring ends and fold the ring ends up to 90 degrees as shown.

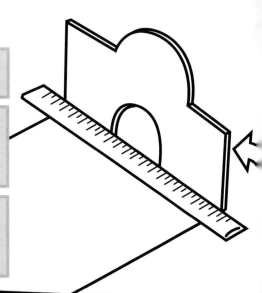

STEP 4

▶ Print out each of the ring cover files onto sheets of white paper and glue to your ring base to make a ring cover.

▶ Print out two copies of ring end B onto your sheets of white paper.

▶ Cut out the shaded area and along the red lines. Glue to the outside ends of the ring as shown here.

STEP 5

▶ Take your piece of string or cord and cut in half.

▶ Take one piece of the string and thread through the top hole on one end of the ring and pull through to the matching hole on the other end of the ring.

▶ Loop the string back through the bottom hole and through to the bottom hole on the other end.

▶ Tighten the string until the ends of the ring are standing up straight, then tie knots in the end of the string and trim off.

STEP 6

▶ Repeat for the other side to complete your ropes.

▶ Place hand through hole in side of ring, find a challenger and prepare to throwdown in your very own TWF ring!

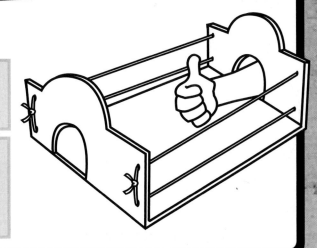

PLANK

We all know that not all matches in the TWF take place in the ring. In fact, when it comes to laying it down and giving your opponent a proper knuckling, there's nothing to beat a handy wooden plank or packing crate to make them really suffer. Copy or trace any of the following pages onto thin cardboard and follow the instructions to lay in a few surprises during your match. Who would expect a bell to come flying in just as your opponent is about to go for his match-winning pin?

Remember, be careful when cutting anything out. If in doubt, get an adult to help you to avoid damaging those precious thumbs before they get a chance to rise to stardom in the TWF.

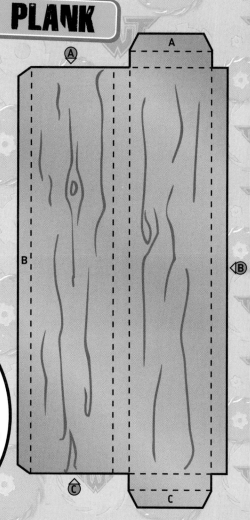

While the Dexteras take a well-earned break and a trip to their local multiplex, it seems those sneaky Sinistras will take any chance they can get to ruin things for everyone.

See if you can spot the Sinistras in the crowd and point them out to the staff to put an end to their popcorn-hurling, movie-ruining mischief.

▷▷▷▷▷▷
ANSWERS
ON PAGE 94

LOCKER-ROOM LAUGHS!

Dick's Puzzle Pages

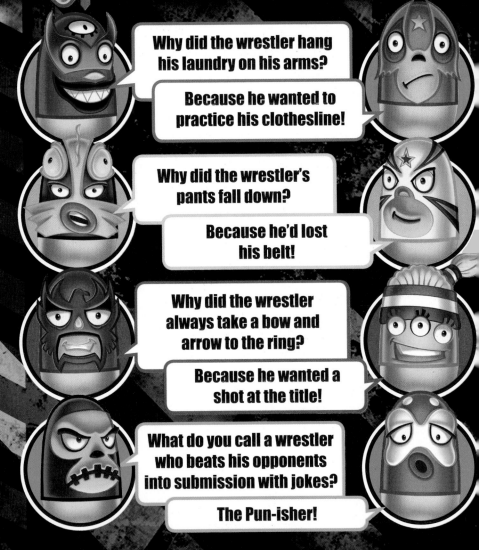

Why did the wrestler hang his laundry on his arms?

Because he wanted to practice his clothesline!

Why did the wrestler's pants fall down?

Because he'd lost his belt!

Why did the wrestler always take a bow and arrow to the ring?

Because he wanted a shot at the title!

What do you call a wrestler who beats his opponents into submission with jokes?

The Pun-isher!

WORDSEARCH

How many can you find?

Look up, down, across, diagonally, and backwards

```
                    A Q P Z
              D C S S D O K A S T
            S F L G D W S C E E L F
            R H G A T H A V U I N U A F
          S T L J I W T Y N H T A B B G D
        A R I Q W R K L N M N S T M J S O S
        S D I N L E L D E O W Y U D A E N Q
        A Z X N I I H R B N O B K X T N K E
    W T D U R G S T I R K T I H A A A E T S
    W W Y F A S N T B A E E T O S B T Y U D
    F F N C U Q O G R M Y M S M H R O A O G
    S S A D E X T E R A S O Y E E O R O S A
    D M H F A W E K G S H E T G C S S M
    N O I T A R E D E F S R E T A K F P
    S D T H W E U R H D F U W K D U T A
    T M U H S Q J O V F R G O I L E
        A M Q T T I Y N H F T T M L
          B E L T Y K S B H K R X
            A E D E T F X J Q A
                I R W Q
```

- [ ] Belt
- [ ] Senator Skull
- [ ] Hometown Huck
- [ ] Corbata
- [ ] N Fuego
- [ ] Dexteras
- [ ] Federation
- [ ] Dwayne Bramage
- [ ] TWF
- [ ] Danny Kaboom
- [ ] Itsy Bitsy
- [ ] Thumb
- [ ] Sinistras
- [ ] Ring
- [ ] Gill

▷▷▷▷▷▷
ANSWERS ON PAGE 94

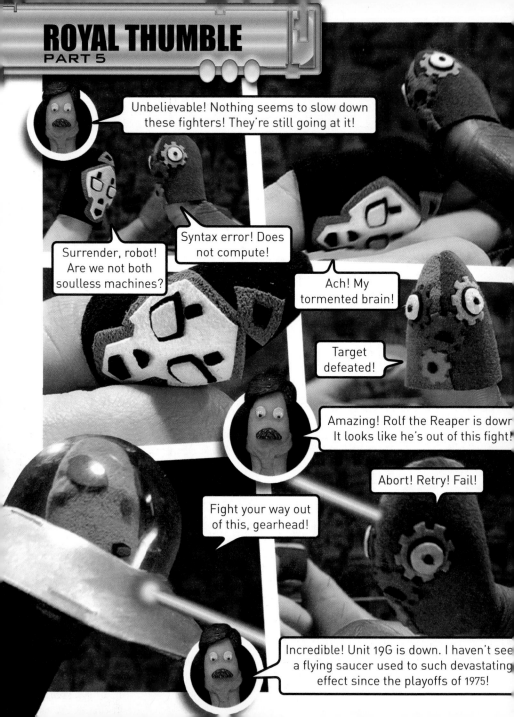

CONTINUED ON PAGE 86

CREATE-A-WRESTLER

Now's your chance to enter the TWF history books yourself. Everyone dreams of mixing it up and knuckling down with the stars of the TWF. With the help of our Thumb Wrestling Federation stylists you can use this simple guide to immortalize your own creations and maybe one day see them lift the TWF belt for themselves.

HEAD BASES

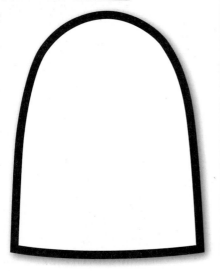

Trace the head base to your left onto a piece of paper and then let your imagination powerslam those colors onto the base to start your creation. Use whatever colors you want. Here are a few examples to get you started.

FACES

STEP 1

Pick a face shape, or make up one of your own and add it to your wrestler. Don't forget, the more colorful the better.

MOUTHS

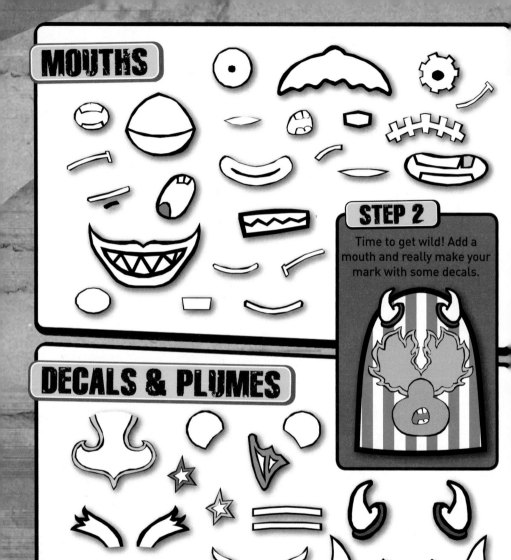

STEP 2

Time to get wild! Add a mouth and really make your mark with some decals.

DECALS & PLUMES

12

EYES

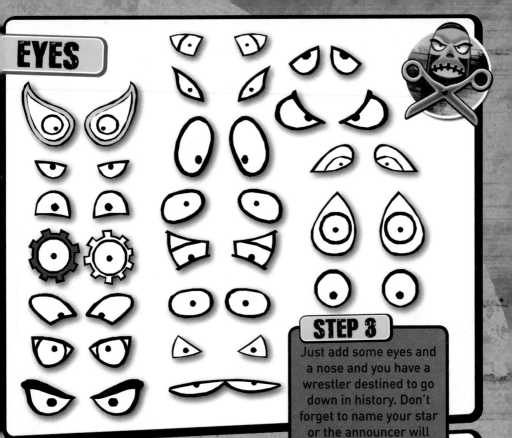

STEP 3

Just add some eyes and a nose and you have a wrestler destined to go down in history. Don't forget to name your star or the announcer will have real problems.

NOSES

WHERE IN THE WORLD?

GREENLA[ND]

NORTH AMERICA

CENTRAL AMERICA

SOUTH AMERICA

Welcome ladies and gentlemen to what would have been another exciting bout from the world of thumb wrestling . . . if all the superstars hadn't gone home that is. As an employee of the TWF you've got to help our talent travel department find where all the wrestlers have gone. Using your knowledge of our stars, draw a line to each of their homes.

VINI VIDI VICTORY

CHEEKO ROJO

GARY THE INTERN

QUEEN NEFERCREEPY

EUROPE

ASIA

CENTRAL ASIA

MIDDLE EAST

AFRICA

AUSTRALIA

SIR SERPENT

N FUEGO

COLONEL COSSACK

KNOCKOUT NINJA

ANSWERS ON PAGE 95

CREATE A LOGO

Ever since my days of wrestling wild bears in Siberia for the last berries on the tree, I have always known that no matter how much crushing you do, you still need a cool logo to put on wooly babushkas for your fans. It's not as hard as it sounds, either. Why don't you have a try using some of the designs given here. Remember to use plenty of color, and if you get stuck, check out the logo that I made. It's cooler than my Aunt Inga's ice box!

▶ It's time to introduce the wrestlers! In your own words, how will the announcer describe them?

HINT!
Don't forget all the wrestlers have their own catchphrases and often try to insult their opponents.

In this corner, for the Mighty Dexteras . . .

And in this corner, for the Sinistras . . .

HINT!
Use some of the wrestling moves shown above, or even make up your own.

▶ The ref starts the match, and both wrestlers chant, "Four, three, two, one! Who will be the strongest thumb?" It's time to thumble! What happens in round one? You decide who will come out ahead, the sneaky Sinistras or those dastardly Dexteras? Draw your action in the ring.

▶ It's on to round two, and after nonstop action the fans are all wondering just what's going to happen next in this edge-of-the-seat match. Is it all a bit one-sided, or are both wrestlers landing some big hits? Only you can decide.

▶ Round two is over. What do Dick and the Colonel have to say about the match so far?

HINT!
Remember that Colonel sometimes seems like he has been watching something else and often says some really silly things!

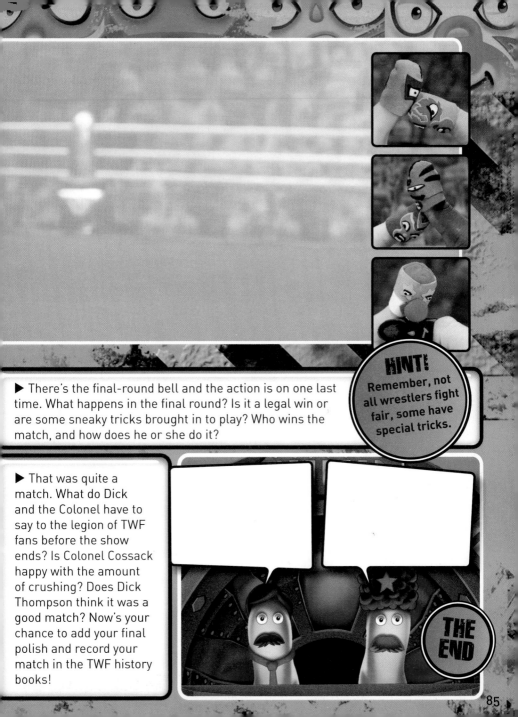

▶ There's the final-round bell and the action is on one last time. What happens in the final round? Is it a legal win or are some sneaky tricks brought in to play? Who wins the match, and how does he or she do it?

HINT!
Remember, not all wrestlers fight fair, some have special tricks.

▶ That was quite a match. What do Dick and the Colonel have to say to the legion of TWF fans before the show ends? Is Colonel Cossack happy with the amount of crushing? Does Dick Thompson think it was a good match? Now's your chance to add your final polish and record your match in the TWF history books!

THE END

DESIGN YOUR OWN WRESTLER

Now's your chance to record your own wrestler in TWF history!

NAME

POWER

AGILITY

STAMINA

PROFILE

NAME

POWER

AGILITY

STAMINA

PROFILE

PROFILE

STATISTICS

POWER

AGILITY

STAMINA

DEXTERAS

STATISTICS

POWER

AGILITY

STAMINA

PROFILE

NAME

POWER
AGILITY
STAMINA

PROFILE

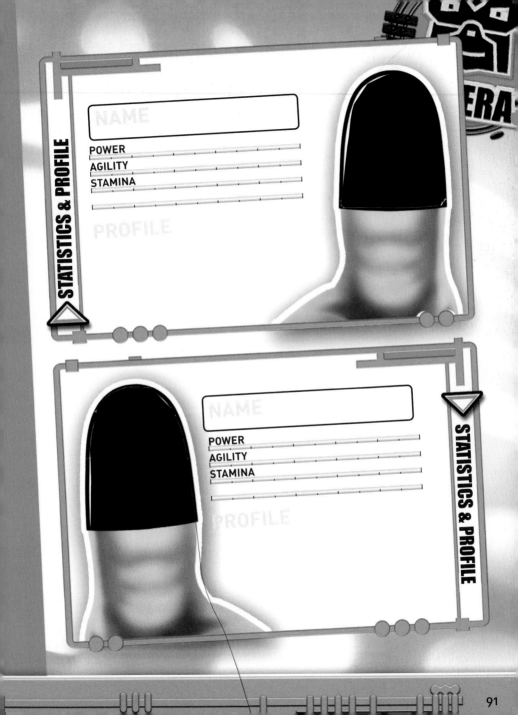

NAME

POWER
AGILITY
STAMINA

PROFILE

17 TWF TEASERS

1 Senator Skull

2 Wasabi

3 Hometown Huck and Big Star

4 Big Bad Billy Goatetsky

5 Colonel Cossack

26

Crossword solution:

- 1 (down) H O M E T O W N H U C K
- 2 (across) C O L O N E L C O S S [ ]
- 3 (down) D E X T E R A S [ ]
- 4 (across) T H U M B W R E S [ ]
- 7 (across) S E N A T O [ ]
- 8 (across) R I N G
- 9 (across) G I L L
- 10 (across) I T S Y B I T S Y
- G I N S T R A
- S H O W D O W N
- G O

ANSWERS

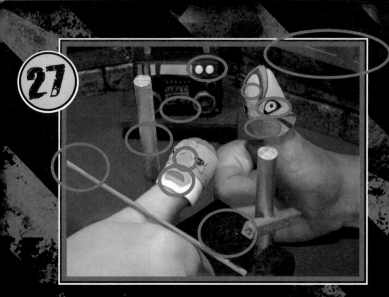

27

54 TWF TEASERS

1. Gill
2. Vini Vidi Victory
3. Big Star
4. Pei Pei the Purple Panda and Laughing Loony
5. Itsy Bitsy

55

E

F

G

ANSWERS

68

71

```
        A Q P Z
      D C S S D O K A S T
      S F L G D W S C E E L F
    R H G A T H A V U I N U A F
    S T L J I W T Y N H T A B B G D
  A R I Q W R K L N M N S T M J E O S
  S D I N I F L D E O W Y U A E N Q
    A Z X N I I H R B N O B K X T A U K E
  W T D U R G S I R K T I H A A E T S
  W W Y F A S N T B A E E T O S B T Y U D
  F F N C U Q O G R M Y M S M H R O A O G
  S S A D E X T E R A S O Y E E O R O S A
    D M H F A W E K G S H E T G C S S M
    N O I T A R E D E F S R E T A K F P
    S D T H W E U R H D F U W K D U T A
    T M U H S Q J O V F R G O I L E
      A M Q T T I Y N H F T T M L
      B E L T Y K S B H K R X
      A E D E T F X J Q A
        I R W Q
```

ANSWERS

SIR SERPENT

N FUEGO

COLONEL COSSACK

KNOCKOUT NINJA

GREENLAND

NORTH AMERICA

EUROPE

ASIA

CENTRAL ASIA

AFRICA

MIDDLE EAST

CENTRAL AMERICA

SOUTH AMERICA

AUSTRALIA

VINI VIDI VICTORY

CHEEKO ROJO

GARY THE INTERN

QUEEN NEFERCREEPY